For Joelie
—M. F.

For Anne Ylvisaker, my story-sharing friend,
and for M., R., and C., my storytelling family
—L. S.

Special thanks to my husband, Matthew Smith,
for always arriving to my studio just in time with patience, insight, and encouragement.
And more special thanks to my Beach Lane editors,
Allyn Johnston and Andrea Welch,
who work wonders with scissors and glue sticks!
—L. S.

Beach Lane Books · An imprint of Simon & Schuster Children's Publishing Division · 1230 Avenue of the Americas, New York, New York 10020 · Text copyright © 2012 by Mem Fox · Illustrations copyright © 2012 by Lauren Stringer · All rights reserved, including the right of reproduction in whole or in part in any form. · BEACH LANE BOOKS is a trademark of Simon & Schuster, Inc. · For information about special discounts for bulk purchases, please contact Simon & Schuster Special Sales at 1-866-506-1949 or business@simonandschuster.com. · The Simon & Schuster Speakers Bureau can bring authors to your live event. For more information or to book an event, contact the Simon & Schuster Speakers Bureau at 1-866-248-8049 or visit our website at www.simonspeakers.com. · Book design by Lauren Rille · The text for this book is set in Colwell. · The illustrations for this book are rendered in acrylic paint on gessoed Arches 140-lb. hot press watercolor paper. · Manufactured in China · 1212 SCP

2 4 6 8 10 9 7 5 3
Library of Congress Cataloging-in-Publication Data
Fox, Mem, 1946–
Tell me about your day today / Mem Fox ; illustrated by Lauren Stringer.—1st ed.
p. cm.
Summary: "What could be more wonderful than sharing bedtime with beloved friends? This little boy loves to talk to his stuffed animals at the end of the day, and share with them all the things that happened to him that day—and to hear about their day, too"—Provided by publisher.
ISBN 978-1-4169-9006-2 (hardback)
ISBN 978-1-4391-5723-7 (eBook)
[1. Bedtime—Fiction. 2. Toys—Fiction. 3. Imagination—Fiction.] I. Stringer, Lauren, ill. II. Title.
PZ7.F8373Te 2012
[E]—dc23
2011058017

# Tell Me About Your Day Today

by Mem Fox · illustrated by Lauren Stringer

Beach Lane Books

New York · London · Toronto · Sydney · New Delhi

There was once a boy who loved bedtime.

He loved the last kiss.

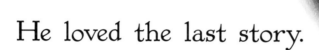

He loved the last story.

He loved the last good night.

He knew he was in the company
of friends and couldn't wait
for their conversation
to begin.

Greedy Goose coughed a little cough.

"Hello, Greedy Goose," the boy whispered. He *loved* Greedy Goose. "Tell me about your day today."

And Greedy Goose
told him about her day~

the who,

the what,

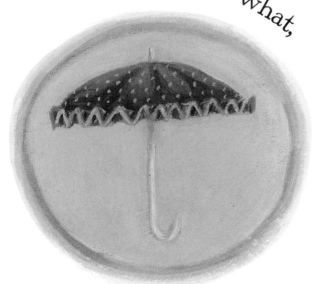

the why,

and the way . . .

the whole wild thing . . .

turned out okay.

Then Blue Horse shook her mane.
"Hello, Blue Horse," the boy whispered.
He *loved* Blue Horse. "Tell me about your
day today."

And Blue Horse told
him about her day~

the who,

the what,

the why,

and the way . . .

the whole wild thing . . .

turned out okay.

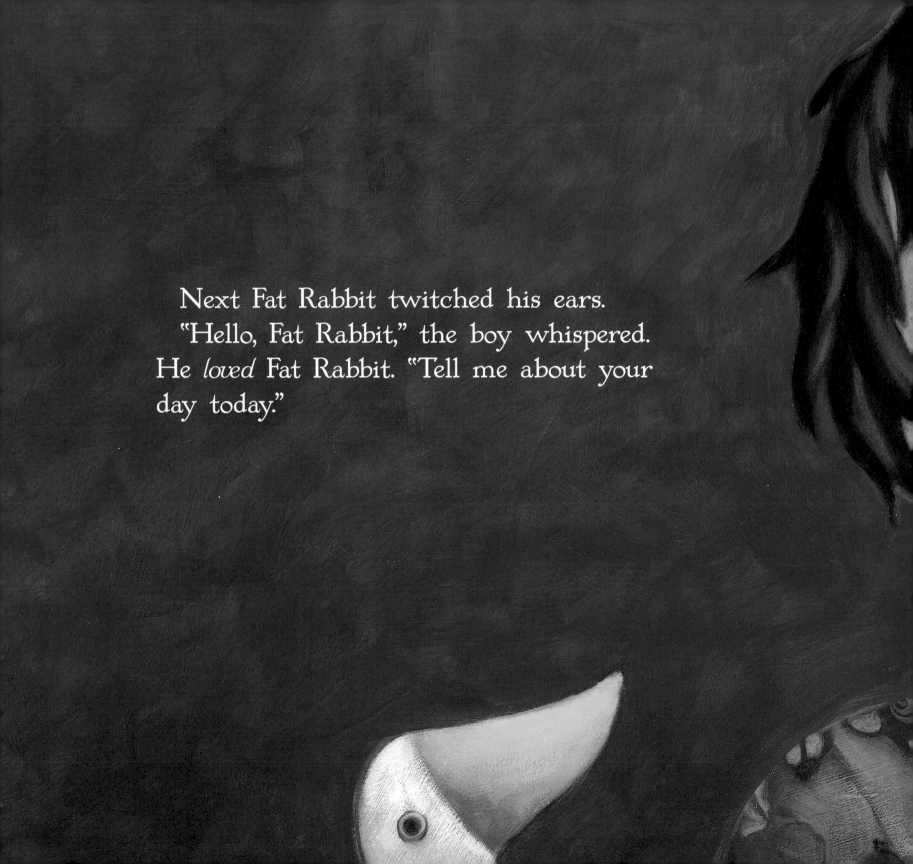

Next Fat Rabbit twitched his ears. "Hello, Fat Rabbit," the boy whispered. He *loved* Fat Rabbit. "Tell me about your day today."

And Fat Rabbit told
him about his day—

the who,

the what,

the why,

and the way . . .

the whole wild thing . . .
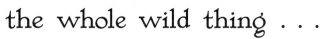

turned out okay.

"But how about you?"
Greedy Goose asked.
"Tell us about *your* day today."

And so the boy looked back . . .

on the who,

the what,

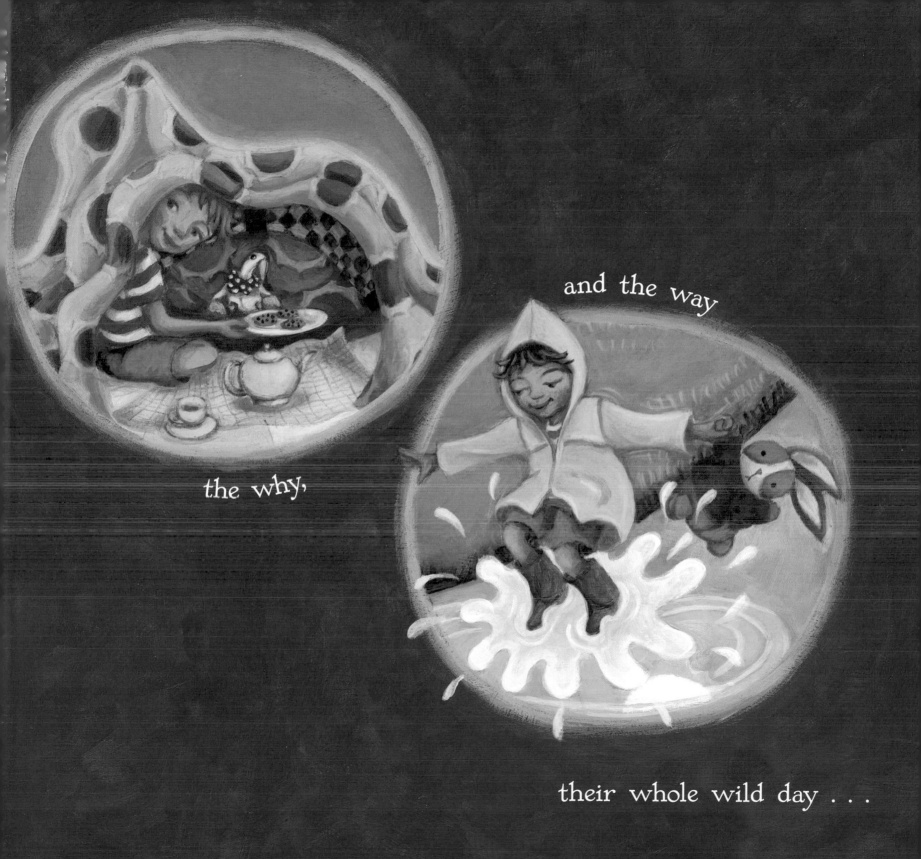

the why,

and the way

their whole wild day . . .

turned out okay!

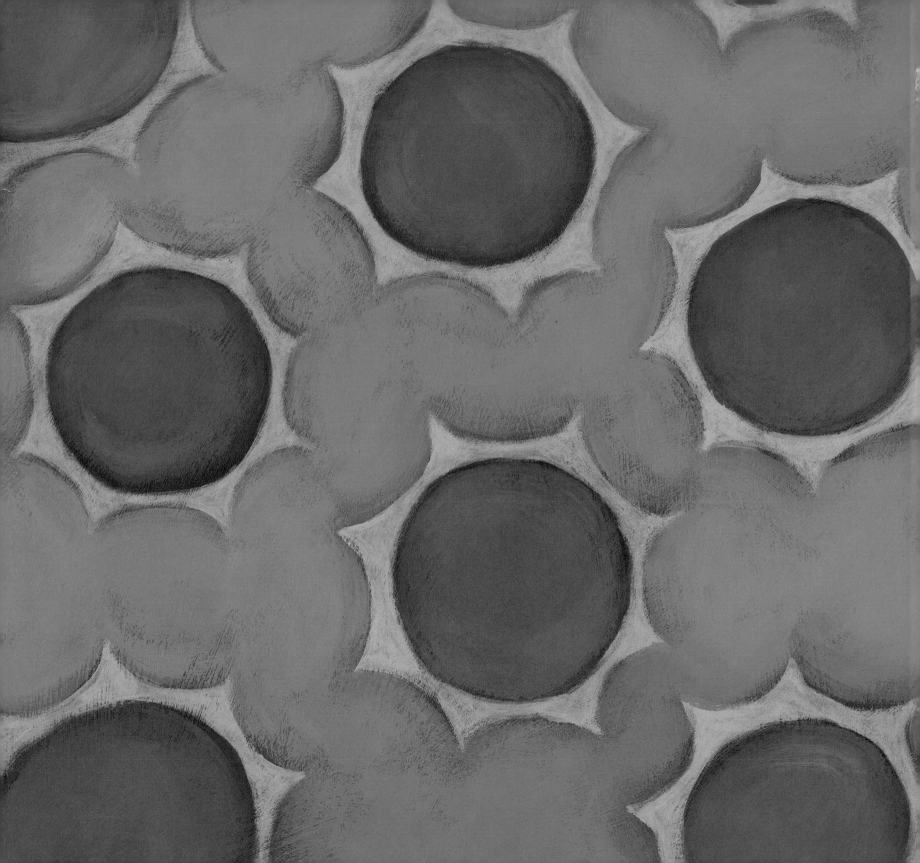